Clara: From Victorian Governess to Lady of Pleasure

Dorian Shellan

Published by Haines Communications, 2023.

This is a work of fiction. Similarities to real people, places, or events are entirely coincidental.

CLARA: FROM VICTORIAN GOVERNESS TO LADY OF PLEASURE

First edition. December 20, 2023.

ISBN: 978-1637860328

Written by Dorian Shellan.

Table of Contents

Clara: From Victorian Governess to Lady of Pleasure

by Dorian Shellan

Chapter One: Clara's Awakening

Ralph Stevens was a stern, austere man, usually very silent and reserved. His wife had died twenty years prior, shortly after giving birth to Clara, and she and her brother, Clarence, were neglected and left to get through their childhood's days as best as they could. When each child attained the age of eleven they were each sent to boarding schools, so while their father had no interest in them he did not spare any expense in ensuring that they were properly educated. Neither Clara nor Clarence could ever remember seeing their father even smile. A continual gloom hung over him, and he usually kept himself locked in his room except at meal times. It came as no surprise to either of them that they should learn of his demise by his own hand, and brother and sister sat quietly at the desk in his study while Mr, Herbert, their father's lawyer, revealed the contents of the deceased's will to them.

Clarence was the sole beneficiary of the estate, with the provision that Clara could remain at the house for as long as she wished. However, despite being entitled to a rather carefree life, for her late father's wealth provided every luxury that she could wish for, she found continued living there to be rather boring, and she resolved to make an effort to leave it.

One day she went to Clarence and expressed a wish to take a situation as a governess. Such a position would place her in society and provide her with the ability to use her education. Clarence made only cursory objections and granted his consent quite readily.

Clara immediately sent an advertisement to the London papers and received several answers. Among them was one from a Mr. Herbert Chester who lived in a most fashionable area of the city. He offered such advantageous terms that Clara at once accepted them, and the next day started for her new home.

Clara was met at the door of the house by the owner, a handsome man of about thirty-five years of age. He introduced her to his wife, a confined invalid who never left her chamber, and then to the children who were to be her pupils. They were two little girls of six and seven years of age.

The residence was fitted up with all the elegance wealth could command. The grounds were handsomely laid out, the gardens cultivated to the extreme of art, and in short, it bore resemblance to the residences which are occupied by the aristocracy. It was also in close proximity to the park, where Clara would take the children for a daily stroll and give them opportunity to play. There, she would also meet other governesses with whom she could engage in conversation more fitting to adults.

Mrs. Chester never interfered with Clara's involvement with the children, and most days passed without her even seeing the mistress of the house, since she preferred to take her meals in her room.

Mr. Chester was a perfect gentleman, courteous, polite and agreeable, and Clara soon felt quite at home with him. As governess, Clara was naturally thrown much into his society, and it did not escape her notice that he grew more and more tender towards her. When shaking hands he would press her hand and retain it in his, and when she wore a low-necked dress at dinner his eyes fixed on her white shoulders. When she leaned forward and he caught a glimpse of her bosom, his face would flush. Clara felt sorry for his having such a sick wife, for it was easy to be seen that he was a man of a very amorous temperament, and it was also certain that his wife could afford him no satisfaction in this respect. Poor Mr. Chester was debarred from those sexual enjoyments of which she felt assured he must be very fond.

One day, Clara stumbled in an obscure corner of the library on some amorous books. Securing them and conveying them to her chamber, she then examined them and found that they contained pictures of a very lascivious character. In fact men and women, as naked as they were born, were performing the sexual act. Her ideas up to that time were very vague regarding sex, but she was determined to become fully enlightened in these matters. She read the books repeatedly, and they soon made her adept in sexual knowledge. Excited by their contents, she became given to secret self-satisfaction, for want of an actual awakening.

On a summer evening when Mr. Chester had gone to his club and the children were asleep, Clara entered the drawing room with one of those prizes in her hand, determined to enjoy it all to herself. She soon fell into a state of delicious languor and, throwing herself carelessly on the sofa while reading the book. She was wearing a low-necked dress, and the weather being warm, had unfastened three of the top loops, thus leaving a considerable portion of her breasts exposed. As she read, her cheeks became flushed, her bosom heaved, and her dress became disarranged, revealing a considerable portion of her limbs as her fingers strove for contentment. She was altogether in a state propitious for an attack when she was suddenly startled by the sound of a voice at her elbow. "What is the name of that book which seems to engross so much of your attention?" Asked the voice.

She looked up to see Mr. Chester himself gazing on her with heightened color and burning eyes.

"Mister Chester," she gasped. Quickly raising herself from the seat, revealing by this movement a considerable portion of her legs and even flashed a glimpse of her thighs. "You ought not to come so stealthily into the room."

"My dear girl, you are wrong," he replied. "I did not come here stealthily, but it was your preoccupation which prevented you from hearing me enter." He smiled. "But you have not replied to my question. What book are you reading?"

"Oh, it is a stupid work I found in the library. I have only just glanced at it and do not find it worth reading."

"I believe you should permit me to judge that for myself," he replied, taking a seat beside her.

"Oh no, Mr. Chester. I cannot allow it," she protested, and pressed the book to her bosom.

"Oh, but I insist." He endeavored to snatch the work from her hands, and in the struggle his hand came in contact with her breasts, brushing against and exposing her right nipple before, at last, obtaining possession of the book.

Clara looked imploringly at him, but he opened it deliberately and read the title aloud. "The Memoirs of a Woman of Pleasure." He closed the book and looked down at her. "So. This is the subject of your studies, is it?"

"I assure you I have not read a page of it. It appeared to me foolish and uninteresting, and I was just about to return it to the library when you entered." But her blushing and inability to look her employer in the eye conveyed that Clara was not telling the truth.

Mr. Chester put the book down on the end table and wrapped his left arm around Clara's shoulders while his right hand maneuvered onto her left breast. "You may call me Herbert," he told her, then pressed his lips into hers.

Clara was confounded and endeavored to escape him, but he held her tightly and continued his attention.

"Herbert, Mr. Chester, this is wrong, let me go." She struggled in vain. "I beg of you."

He replied by pressing another kiss onto Clara's lips, continuing until her struggles subsided and his hand was unencumbered as he fondled her breasts. Unable to hide the pleasure that Herbert's attentions were providing, she began to participate in the kisses and return his caresses. "But we should be done," she murmured between embraces. "For someone might come in."

"My dear, there is no cause for concern. There is no one around but you and I. My wife is confined to her chamber, the servants are downstairs, and the children are fast asleep. We are absolutely alone."

His words caused Clara's whole body became calmer, and she reclined negligently in his arms. Herbert again pressed his lips to hers, and this time inserted the end of his tongue into her mouth. Her response was as ardent as his own.

He then cautiously unhooked her dress, but she made no pretense to restrain him. Her frock fell off her shoulders and her naked bust was entirely exposed to his view. He passed from one to the other of the ivory globes and molded them with his hands, playing with the nipples and applying his lips to them. The contact stoked the fire in her, and she offered no resistance as he eased her back and began to raise her petticoats. Clara's desires now overwhelming her, she was completely in his power. He touched her legs, reached her knees, and at last his hand came in contact with her alabaster thighs. He rested there a moment, continuing to excite her with kisses before becoming more bold.

Her head fell back as his agitated right hand then ascended the inside of her left thigh, until at last he reached the down covering her mossy mound. Running his fingers to her labia lips, he forced one between them and gently rubbed her clitoris. Clara opened her thighs to the widest capacity and absolutely cried out with pleasure at his touch.

Herbert then moved his head down from Clara's palpitating bosom and applied his lips to where he had just placed his hand. He kissed her mons and inserted his tongue between the folding lips, seeking out her clitoris and playing with it at will.

"Oh, what pleasure!" She cried out, now drunk with delirious joy. "Do what you will with me, my dearest Herbert."

His reply was to stand up and divest himself of his clothing while she watched. He then took her hands, and as he eased her to her feet her dress fell around her ankles. They were soon both naked.

Herbert turned Clara round and round, patting her buttocks and caressing her body all over. Neither were her hands idle. She seized his magnificent instrument and gently rubbed it while tickling his scrotum beneath. Both now almost crazed with desire, Herbert reclined her onto her back on the sofa and threw himself on the top.

Clara eagerly opened her thighs to receive him and guided his fiery dart to the entrance of her cunt. He entered the lips and met little resistance as she raised her buttocks and gave a sudden heave upwards. Herbert's instrument was suddenly embedded within the sheath destined by nature to receive it, and he immediately commenced the delicious movements. Clara looked across his back and saw their naked bodies reflected in the mirrors as his cock furiously pounded until at last the moment of no return began. "Oh, Herbert," she screamed while her fingers clawed at his shoulders. "Don't stop, don't stop."

She closed her eyes, her eyelids trembled, and with a convulsive movement she wrapped her legs around his loins and pressed him so tightly that she almost took away his breath. It was then over. She felt his ejaculate rush into her thirsty cunt while at the same moment she succumbed to her own libations. Her hold relaxed, and they both fell all their lengths on the couch.

After remaining without motion a few minutes, Herbert kissed her again, for he was by no means finished with their tryst. He rose from the couch, and then raising her up and placing her on its edge, he again commenced. With one hand he raised one of her arms in the air in such a manner as to leave her breasts entirely at his discretion. He took one of the nipples in his mouth and pressed her to him with his other hand. Clara's thighs were widely separated, and he had no difficulty in entering her vagina. He slightly bent his knees and was soon buried again in the grotto of delight. She assisted him by every means in her power, and in a short time they were again inundated with their mutual emissions.

CLARA'S TIME AS GOVERNESS after the adventure with Mr. Chester passed very agreeably. Her amorous desires were fully satisfied as she frequently enjoyed a repetition of the scenes she had passed through that evening. Herbert was very ardent and very ingenious in his mode of performing the sexual act. Clearly, Clara had become a most suitable replacement for his wife in that regard. However, this time of bliss was not to go unchallenged. One day Clara was informed that Mr. Chester's sister-in-law was coming to spend a few weeks with them. Herbert gave Clara the information with manifest pleasure painted on his face, and she felt sure her coming pleased him. For her part, however, Clara was not especially delighted, for she was afraid the presence of his wife's sister would interfere negatively with their enjoyments.

Chapter Two: Voyeurism and Tribadism

On the appointed day, a carriage drove up to the entrance of the house and Catherine Thorpe, Mrs. Chester's sister, alighted. Clara felt a surge of dismay the moment that she saw her, conjecturing why Herbert may have been so pleased to have her coming to stay with them. Clearly, Catherine was one of the most beautiful women Clara had ever beheld. She was about twenty years of age and above medium height. Her face was lovely, her features faultless, her complexion fair, and yet the hue of health was on her cheek. Her hair was a dark glossy brown and hung in natural ringlets on her snowy neck and shoulders, down to her voluptuous and beautifully rounded breasts.

When they were introduced, Catherine received Clara with a good deal of warmth in her manner. "My," she complimented the governess. "You are a pretty girl, indeed." She smiled at her brother-in-law. "It may be well that I am here, for your being in the house must be quite a temptation for Herbert." She giggled and turned back to Clara. "I am confident that you and I will be good friends."

"Thank you, Miss Thorpe." Clara replied, smiling with a slight nod. "That would be delightful."

The two ladies took tea together that afternoon, and Catherine asked Clara a great many questions concerning

Herbert Chester, as to "how she liked him," "how he behaved towards her," and a number of other interrogatories. Clara began to suspect that she may have a rival for Herbert's attention, but politely answered her questions and insisted that Mr. Chester was always the perfect gentleman.

When she awoke the next morning and went downstairs for breakfast, Clara found that Miss Thorpe already risen and had gone into the garden for a stroll. Since it was already warm and sunny outside and the children had not yet risen, she decided to follow with the intent of joining her. Not seeing her right away, Clara directed her steps to the summer house situated at the bottom of the lawn. The pathway that led to it was grass, so that the sound of footsteps could not be heard. This proved to be most advantageous, for when she approached she heard the rustling of a dress inside. So, instead of opening the door, she peeped through the keyhole. Such a sight befell her that it sent the blood boiling through her veins.

Herbert Chester was reclining on his back on a divan which he had drawn into the middle of the floor. His pantaloons were slipped down to his heels, leaving the whole of the lower portion of his body uncovered. Straddling him, with one foot resting on the ground and with the other on the divan was the beautiful Catherine. Her dress was open in front, leaving her splendid breasts entirely bare. Her petticoats were elevated above her navel and thrown behind her white belly, fully exposing her thighs and magnificent legs. Above all that, since she stood directly facing the door, her lovely mound was entirely exposed to Clara's gaze.

Herbert's instrument then penetrated the luscious lips of Catherine's slit, and while Clara watched he gave a tremendous heave upwards with his buttocks and sent it into her body clear up to his testicles. Catherine was clearly gorged with delight, her face expressing the most intense enjoyment. They commenced to move together, he directing his thrusts upwards while she worked her bottom in reply to his motions.

While this play continued, Clara could distinctly see Herbert's staff entering in and out of her coral sheath, the lips of which embraced it so tightly that they seemed to be afraid it should escape from them. It was the most voluptuous sight she had ever seen.

By the quivering of Catherine's eyelids Clara felt assured the crisis would soon come. As the acme approached, Catherine leaned over and kissed Herbert, their tongues seeking each other's mouths. So intense was their feeling of pleasure that they actually bit each other.

"Dear Herbert, I am coming," the lovely woman suddenly exclaimed.

These words seemed to increase Herbert's ardor, for he commenced to work his bottom with lightning rapidity, and suddenly giving a tremendous push upwards which she replied to by a corresponding motion downwards. Suddenly, they both became motionless, his staff so deeply engulfed in her that the hair of their genitals was intermingled. Convulsive movement then seized Catherine's whole frame and she fell onto his belly. He remained embedded inside her.

They remained still for only a few minutes before Catherine opened her eyes and kissed Herbert repeatedly on the lips. The warmth of her caresses appeared to reanimate him and he returned her embraces. "I must now go, darling," she said. "Someone may come."

"But I must once more taste the delights of heaven," he replied. "We shall have no more opportunity today, dear Catherine, and I am not half satisfied yet." He withdrew himself from her and drew her onto his knee, then began gently to titillate her clitoris with his finger.

Catherine began to wriggle her buttocks in response to his ministrations. "Herbert," she panted. "I shall spend if you continue your titillations much longer."

Herbert responded by sliding her onto her knees on the floor. She performed her part by then taking his lance in her hand and, uncovering the ruby head, passed it between her lips. He slid his hands behind her head, and Clara watched the proceeding fellatio with utmost delight.

They continued this play until the motion of Catherine's mouth evidently brought him nearer to consummation, and he withdrew his member. "Come then, darling," he told her. "I too am ready."

He reclined her on the divan and taking her thighs in his arms, he drove his lance to the hilt into her body. They seemed no longer to know what they were about. Joined as they were together, Catherine especially appeared to be enjoying the utmost voluptuousness. Her rapid movements, her exclamations of supreme pleasure, the trembling of her eyelids, and the convulsive manner in which she pressed Herbert's bottom was sufficient proof of her intense pleasure. After a few more reciprocal motions, they again discharged.

Clara then rose, adjusted her clothing, and thought it best to retire back to the house. She sat in the breakfast room and was drinking a cup of tea when Catherine entered, apparently as fresh as ever. She greeted Clara with a kiss on the cheek and told her that she had been out in the garden, taking a long walk.

Clara did not say a word and suppressed a smile by feigning a sip from her cup. She determined to take her own time to disclose what she had witnessed.

DURING THE FOLLOWING days Clara noticed that Catherine would greet her with a great deal of warmth, kissing and pressing against her, but she thought nothing of it. After all, it seemed that it was in Catherine's nature to be so amorous.

One night, however, as they proceeded upstairs to get ready for bed, their conversation continued into Clara's room. Catherine seated herself on the side of the bed and watched as Clara began to disrobe in order to put her nightgown on. As Clara unhooked the front of her dress it fell open on her shoulders, and her chemise, being open in front, allowed her bosom to become fully exposed.

Catherine's eyes brightened. She stood up, moved behind Clara, and began to mold her hands around Clara's breasts. Although this action somewhat surprised her, Clara made no resistance. Rather, she felt the contact of soft hands caressing her breasts to be very agreeable.

"What delicious breasts you have," said Catherine. "How well formed they are. See how stiff your rosy nipples stand out from this field of snow. Oh, how I would love to kiss and press them." She moved in front of Clara and buried her head between the two globes. "And then your belly," she continued, passing her hand over it. "How soft and white it is." How happy will the man be who presses that belly to his own?"

"Oh, Catherine, you should not talk in that manner," Clara replied, her face flushing with the fire kindled by Catherine's lascivious touching. "I am certain that you exaggerate. My breasts are smaller than yours, and I doubt they are more firm."

"Well, come then. Let us compare them." Catherine replied as she unhooked her own dress and pulled it down to her waist.

Her breasts completely exposed, Clara tentatively reached out to touch them. They were beautifully formed. So firm and elastic, and standing boldly out from her chest. She pressed and caressed them, then after Catherine nudged the back of her head to push her forward she began to suck the rosy nipples which stood out stiff with desire.

"Come," said Catherine. "Let us rub our breasts together, for I am sure it will give us mutual delight."

Clara's eyes moved up to meet Catherine's. "I will do anything you wish," she murmured. "For I feel a strange fire burning in me."

Both women pulled down clothes as low as possible and brought their chests together in such a way that their breasts rubbed against each other. "Is it not exquisite?" Catherine whispered. "The sensations of your breast against mine fires my whole blood."

"I experience the same feelings," Clara admitted. This strange action fueling amorous sensations within her.

"Clara?" Catherine asked after a few minutes repose. Do you know what I would like to do?"

"Please tell me."

"I should like to explore your more secret beauties."

"With all my heart," Clara replied instantly, "But you must allow me the same privilege."

"Most willingly. I should love that indeed," Catherine responded.

"Come then," Clara exclaimed. "For I feel most ready for you do with me as you like."

"Dear girl, how good we are going to feel." Catherine told her. "Lie down with your belly on the bed, then keep still for me so that I may admire and manipulate your beauty."

Clara excitedly threw herself face down on the bed while Catherine came behind her and lifted up her petticoats, exposing Clara's bottom to her gaze. She smiled as she gazed at the pouting lips of Clara's vagina, faintly overshadowed with hair, between her inner thighs. She moved Clara's legs slightly apart, by which movement the lips of her sheath were separated, revealing a line of coral between them.

"Does this position suit you, Catherine?" Clara asked with her face buried in the bed.

"Absolutely! It is a most charming position indeed," Catherine replied while molding and pressing Clara's buttocks. She then leaned forward and covered them with the most lascivious and ardent nibbles and kisses. "And so delicious," she continued.

"Catherine, Catherine!" Clara exclaimed as she began to squirm. "You are killing me with pleasure."

"Oh Clara, how the sight of your beauty fires me. What magnificent buttocks you possess. How white and firm, and how well developed they are." She again bent down to continue smothering them with kisses. "I should never be tired kissing your lovely bottom," she continued. "And the edges of that dear little cleft I see between your thighs, how inviting it looks. How beautiful it is, shaded with such silky down. Oh, I must. I must,"

She said as she put her finger between the lips of Clara's sheath and titillated her vagina. "So charming, so delicious," she repeated.

"Oh Catherine, I am in a blaze. My slit is on fire."

"See how deliciously tight your vagina clasps my finger, and what a delightful warmth is there. There! Now I have your clitoris! How stiff it is!"

"Dearest Catherine," Clara exclaimed, wiggling her buttocks, for the in-and-out motion of Catherine's finger was more than she could bear. "Your touching and titillations are bringing on a crisis. Stay the motion of your finger or I shall come. Oh, there. Oh there it is! Oh my." Clara uncontrollably moved her buttocks up and down, imitating the conjugal act, while Catherine continued her manipulations until the crisis came. Clara then fell motionless again, flat on her belly, as Catherine slowly withdrew her dripping finger from Clara's sheath. She remained in this recumbent posture for several minutes before slowly rolling over and smiling up at her companion. "Wow!"

"'Come now, Clara," Catherine said. "For heaven's sake, you must give me relief, for I am so aroused."

Clara slid off the bed, and seizing Catherine by the waist, pushed her down onto it. She fell on her back and Clara threw her petticoats over her head, revealing all the lower portion of Catherine's body. What a beautiful sight it was. Two magnificently developed thighs led up to a charming grotto covered with wispy hair, between the pouting lips of which could be seen her clitoris, stiff with intense desire. Clara admired for a moment Catherine's beauties, and then commenced her manipulations. First, she stroked her belly, implanting kiss after kiss upon it. She then played with the hair covering her mound, twisting her finger in and out of it, before dividing the lips of her sheath and titillating her highly excited clitoris.

"Great Heavens, Catherine," she exclaimed. "What a beautiful cunt you have. What delicious pouting lips, surrounded so teasingly with downy hair. And then your clitoris, how finely developed. I cannot help but kiss it." Clara stooped down and inserted her tongue between the lips of Catherine's ruby passage, titillating her clitoris with the tip of it, then looked up at into Catherine's liquid eyes.

"'Clara, darling, keep on. Keep on." Catherine blurted out, almost crazed with delight."

"Then I shall also suck it." Her mouth descended, sucking and licking. "How delicious," she exclaimed between breaths.

Catherine opened her thighs to the widest extent and lifted her legs high in the air. A convulsive shudder ran through her frame and she discharged profusely, appearing to be perfectly annihilated by the deliciousness of her sensations.

Clara eased herself by her side on the bed, and after a long pause they both rose and kissed each other tenderly. Such was Clara's initiation in the sport of tribadism.

Chapter Three: Threesome

During the following days Clara and Catherine spent as much time together as Clara's duties permitted. They read amorous books and filled quiet intervals with tender conversation. Clara found Catherine to be a very intelligent girl who conversed easily on almost every subject.

One day they decided they would sleep together, and forgoing sleepwear they both slept naked. Clara woke up during that night and turned to Catherine, who was sound asleep. Her beautiful hair covered the pillow like a veil. Her ruby lips were slightly separated, revealing her pearly teeth, and her cheeks were tinged with a slight color which made her appear most lovely. Feeling playful, Clara eased down the bedclothes until Catherine's breasts were exposed. They were firm, round and white as the driven snow, and surmounted by delicate pink nipples.

Smiling, and becoming aroused, Clara continued to fold back the blanket and sheet. Catherine's magnificently molded thighs were stretched widely apart, and at the lower part of her belly was her glorious domain of Venus. A very pretty cunt, indeed. Staring at the hillock surmounted with delicate curls, between which could be seen the pouting lips to the entrance of bliss, folded so closely together that only a line of coral showed where they joined, it was a sight too inviting to ignore. Unable to resist, she leaned over and imprinted a kiss on that fountain of delight, then gently divided the lips with her finger. Seeking out the clitoris, she soon had it swelling under her touches. In a few moments it grew quite stiff.

A shiver of delight ran through Catherine's frame, but she did not wake. With a finger of her other hand, Clara penetrated into the coral passage and began to move it rapidly in and out of her vagina, while with her other finger she continued to titillate Catherine's clitoris.

Still asleep, Catherine responded to these ministrations by working her bottom up and down. "Oh Herbert," she exclaimed. "It is too delightful! Faster darling, faster."

Clara moved her finger faster. She could feel the vaginal muscles begin to contract on it, while Catherine wiggled herself to and fro. She called out, "I am coming, darling, dear Herbert, I am com...com..." But she could utter no more. Pushing her mound close up to Clara's hand, Clara felt her fingers endowed with the love potion she had distilled from her. At the moment of discharging she awoke, and, opening her eyes, gazed with astonishment. "Is it you, dear Clara?" She exclaimed as soon as she could recover her breath. "I really thought it was..." She seemed suddenly to remember and hesitated to finish her sentence.

"You thought it was Herbert Chester."

Catherine blushed and bit her lower lip, but made no verbal reply.

"I saw your proceedings with him in the summer house," Clara continued. "But do not be alarmed, dear Catherine, for I am willing to keep it in confidence."

"Did you enjoy watching us?"

"I did." Clara smirked. "I suspect I may be somewhat of a voyeur."

"Then, perhaps, since you promise discretion, I may arrange it so you may do so again. Would you like that?"

"Oh, very much so."

"But first," Catherine said as she raised up from her reclining posture. She seized Clara by the waist and pushed her down onto the bed. "Since you have given me the most intense enjoyment this morning, I am going to be equally kind to you." Then, uttering exclamations of pleasure, she began to run her hands rapidly over Clara's naked body while kissing her breasts. Her right hand smoothed across her belly and descended down to Clara's very center of pleasure.

Clara stretched back and raised her pubis in response.

Running her fingers through the pubic hair, Catherine parted the lips and slid a finger against the ruby cavity between. She then seized on Clara's clitoris, exciting it with her lascivious touches, and at last, as if unable to control herself longer, she forced a finger into the deepest recesses of Clara's vagina and commenced to move it rapidly in and out. Suddenly, she desisted from her manipulations. "Stay here, just like that," she said, reaching into the nightstand drawer. She took from it a rubber dildo, shaped exactly like a man's instrument. "I have something that will give you even greater delight. This is what I amuse myself with when alone," she explained. "And now I am going to give you a taste of it. Place yourself on your knees dear Clara, and recline your head on the pillow."

Clara obediently placed herself in the position she indicated, by which means her buttocks were elevated high in the air.

"How glorious you look in this position, Clara," said Catherine, pressing her hands over her bottom. "What a pretty object your cunt is between your swelling thighs. How closely the plump lips come together and how delicately they are shaded by your curling hair. I must kiss it."

So saying, she stooped down and imprinted a long kiss on the object of her desire. Then Clara felt Catherine's tongue divide the portals and penetrate into the recesses, rendering her wild with the delicious titillation. Clearly, Catherine enjoyed one of her own sex almost as much as she did one of the male kind. She moved her tongue rapidly for a few moments until Clara was about to spend in her mouth. But then she suddenly ceased. "Now, darling, for something more substantial," she exclaimed excitedly, and bringing the point of the dildo to the entrance of Clara's vagina, she plunged it to the very hilt into her glowing sheath. She held it in that position for a full minute, then commenced to move it in and out somewhat slowly, as if for the purpose of prolonging her exquisite feelings. Soon, however, she saw by the motion of Clara's buttocks that she was on the eve of discharging, and placing her hand between her thighs, she titillated both clitoris and bottom at the same moment. With the other hand she drove the dildo with lightning rapidity in and out of the lustful cavity.

Clara could hold out no longer. "I must come, dearest Catherine," she gasped. "There, the..." And with a half murmured ejaculation of pleasure she poured down a flood of juices and sank motionless on her belly in the bed.

Minutes later they both lay side by side, again and again tasting the bliss of the other, until they were unable to do anything more and fell asleep in each other's arms.

AS THEY GATHERED FOR dinner that evening, Catherine whispered to Clara that Herbert had agreed that she could watch him and Catherine together that evening in his room. The three of them then sat down to a delicious repast during which Herbert liberally poured the wine. By the time they finished the third bottle, all eyes were a sparkle and both tongues and inhibitions had been loosened.

"My dear Clara," Herbert began. "Catherine has informed me that you have come to a good understanding together, and I need not tell you how much gratified I am to hear it."

Clara and Catherine looked at each other, both sporting grins.

"But," he addressed them both. "Rather than limiting Clara to simply watching, surely there is no reason we should not enjoy pleasure all together? You are both such beautiful girls, and I believe I can satisfy you both." He watched their expressions. "What do you say, Catherine, do you consent to inviting Clara to bed with us?"

"I shall like it, if it will please you," replied his sister-in-law, a little tentatively, her eyes flitting between Herbert and Clara. It suddenly dawned on her that this might not be Clara's first time with him.

"Then I propose that this evening shall be our initiation." Herbert was most enthusiastic. "Do you consent, Clara?"

"Oh, most willingly," Clara replied eagerly.

"Splendid! Let us finish our dessert and proceed upstairs." He rose from the table. "Follow me, and I will conduct you both to the room destined to be the theater of our joys."

Herbert opened his bedroom door and bade the women inside. It was perfectly certain from their sparkling eyes, heightened color, and from their trembling limbs that they were both aflame with desire; that they were ready to do anything to appease their passions. Still, there was for a moment or two a kind of restraint as to who should begin.

"We have come here to enjoy ourselves," Herbert spoke first. He wrapped his right arm around Catherine, pulling her into a kiss, then took Clara in his left arm. At first he alternated between kissing them, then coaxed them into kissing each other and eased back. "Let us lose no time," he said, smiling broadly. "I propose the first thing we do is for you both to strip each other entirely naked." He settled into an armchair to watch them.

"Oh yes. That would be delightful," Clara said in return, then commenced to unfasten Catherine's frock. They watched their forms reflected in the mirror, and after a few frenzied moments they were both divested of every particle of clothing. Then, hands clasped together, they stood naked in front of Herbert.

Herbert rose to his feet, took both of them in his arms, and led them to the bed. He kissed them all over, while at the same time removing his own clothes. First it was their breasts, then it was their bellies, then it was the centers of love itself, until they were all so excited that the consummation could no longer be delayed. Catherine was beyond herself, for she threw herself on her back on the bed and, opening her white thighs to the widest extent, begged for someone to come and give her relief. "If someone does not come and quench the fire burning in me, I shall die," she moaned. "My slit is on fire. Come Herbert. Come and drive your delicious peg into my vitals. See," she spread her pussy lips apart with her fingers. “I open the door for you. Come, darling, come."

Clara and Herbert watched the voluptuous girl, with her nimble fingers, open the lips of her coral sheath and show them the pink interior. Who could resist such an appeal as this? Certainly not Herbert, for he rushed to the suffering girl and in a moment his cock invaded the mouth of her cunt and, almost instantly, became embedded to the very hair of her salacious cavity. What a delicious sight it was for Clara. She gazed on as Catherine folded her legs and thighs around Herbert’s loins and jutted her pelvis to meet his thrusts.

Suddenly Catherine called out. "Come here, Clara. You must have your share too. Turn your bottom towards me and straddle across my face."

Clara did as she requested, positioning herself such that her notch came directly over Catherine’s mouth.

"Now, Herbert," Catherine continued, "I will titillate Clara’s clitoris with my tongue while you continue to fuck me."

Clara threw her arms around Herbert's neck, and as their faces met his tongue penetrated her lips. In the meantime, she felt Catherine's tongue dancing upon her clitoris in the most entrancing manner.

Herbert began to drive most furiously into Catherine’s body while she kept time with her tongue in Clara’s slit. All were much too excited to be able to prolong this scene, however. Catherine's hot cunt received Herbert's boiling sperm while she responded in such profusion that it actually ran down her white thighs. Nor was Clara far behind, for Catherine's tongue brought down from her a copious shower.

This excitement then over, all three then took a bath together in a wonderfully oversized tub, which was conveniently situated in an adjoining chamber. They then returned to the bedroom to partake of a few glasses of champagne while resting on the divan.

It was almost an hour later when Herbert put his glass down and stood up. "Come, dear Clara," he said, taking her by the hand. "It is your turn now." He laid himself on his back on the bed and drew her up on top of him. In a moment his engine of love had penetrated her slit, rubbing the inside of her already sensitive vagina. Catherine stationed herself behind and watched with flushing eyes and heightened color the in-and-out motion of his rigidity into Clara's body. At last, unable to control herself any longer she passed one hand between their bellies and titillated Clara's clitoris, while with her other hand she tickled alternately her bottom and Herbert's testicles. Soon, however, she changed her tactics and applied some vigorous slaps to Clara's broad buttocks, turning the white cheeks into a rosy hue. Each time she struck it seemed to impale Clara on his fiery staff, causing it to enter a prodigious way inside her.

Insisting that Herbert should remain perfectly passive while she did all the work, Clara moved her buttocks in fine style. The mirror reflected their actions, and not only was she feeling gratified but, owing to their position, she could see his weapon entering in and out of her. It was a delicious sight, enhancing her pleasure tenfold, but also assuring that she could hold back no longer. "I am coming, dear Herbert," she exclaimed. "Spend at the same time that I do."

Herbert, responding to her invocation, suddenly heaved up his buttocks and placed his two hands on her bottom. He pressed her closely to himself and she felt his hot semen rush into her, meeting her own copious discharge.

They then relaxed for a half an hour's enjoyment of more wine during which Herbert's erect weapon, which Clara and Catherine had never ceased handling, showed them that he was again ready for action. This time he devised a new mode for satisfying his desires. He first required Catherine, then Clara, to each take his shaft deep into her mouth, as far as they were able, to show him who could take it the deepest. After proclaiming Clara to be the winner of this little contest, he had Catherine lie down and positioned his scrotum over her mouth, ordering her to suck and lick it, while forcing Clara's head down onto his cock and telling her to take it back and forth in her mouth and throat. They both performed such an exemplary job at their tasks that after only a few minutes his body shuddered, froze, and Clara obediently swallowed his ejaculate.

After a few minutes of rest, Herbert had Catherine lie down lengthwise on the bed and made Clara lie on the top of her with her head between Catherine's thighs. In this position. Clara's mouth came in contact with Catherine's quivering slit while Catherine's mouth did the same with Clara's. As she supported herself on her knees, Clara's bottom was raised perfectly for Herbert to enter her from behind. With Herbert's staff pounding into Clara's cunt and Catherine's tongue dancing on her clitoris, she wildly nibbled and sucked at Catherine's voluptuous cunt until all parties exploded in delight. Then, now quite exhausted, they all reclined on the divan together to relax and drink more wine.

Catherine intently watched Herbert's interactions with his employee. The fact that Herbert had paid more attention to

Clara, fucking her a second time while she only received oral, had initiated a jealous streak in Catherine. Clearly, employee and employer had an amorous history. Did Herbert prefer Clara? Was Catherine's plan to fill in the gap with Herbert after her ailing sister passed in jeopardy? She smiled. This would be resolved within a day. Herbert was certain to want to avoid scandal, and governesses come and go all the time.

Chapter Four: Madame Q's Solution

Clara sat on a bench in the park and watched the squirrels darting back and forth across the lawn. It had been a week since she had left the employ of the Chester household and she was still uncertain as to what to do next. Herbert has assuaged any guilt he might have felt in her dismissal with a severance of twenty-five pounds, almost a year's salary, and a glowing letter of reference. The money had provided her with time to consider her options, so rather than return to the family home she remained in London and took a room in a hotel. The combination of living in a grand house in the city and her recent sexual awakenings had created an ambition in Clara such that returning to the boredom of life in the old family country home was not even an option for her. Neither was further employment as a governess. It was doubtful that any future employer would be as exciting at Herbert Chester had been, but she wanted more from life anyway. She desired the proper life befitting a lady of her breeding and education, along with partaking in the pleasures that London offered.

Clara was so caught up in her musing that she failed to notice the immaculately dressed woman approach until she addressed her. "Good afternoon, Clara," she said in a friendly voice.

Clara suddenly looked up. "Hello, Anna," she replied, rising from the bench. Anna was often in the park and Clara assumed her to be a lady of leisure, either married or having wealth in her own right. They had conversed many times on a variety of subjects, and Clara had always enjoyed her company. "What a beautiful day for a stroll."

"Indeed!" Anna smiled. "May I sit with you?"

"Of course."

"I observe you are not with your charges today?" Anna placed her right hand, delicately encased in a lace glove, on Clara's forearm. "And neither yesterday. Is everything all right?"

"Oh, all is fine, Anna. Mrs. Chester's sister has come to live in the house, so the family had no more need of my services."

"The aunt is to assume the role of governess?" Anna retrieved her hand, and her expression clearly indicated that she did not believe what she was being told.

"No," Clara slowly shook her head, clearly embarrassed. "No, she is not." Her eyes flitted up to meet Anna's. "May I take you into my confidence?"

"But of course." Anna rose and extended her hand. "Come, let us adjourn to Hudson's tea room where we might converse in a more appropriate setting.

Anna's inquisitive and genuinely friendly demeanor soon had Clara telling her everything that had happened, neither disguising nor omitting anything. It felt so good for Clara to talk about it.

Anna listened intently, and her eyes sparkled particularly when Clara depicted her sexual escapades. "What do you plan to do now?" She asked.

"Well," Clara began as she carefully returned the china cup to its saucer. "I am left with the necessity upon me of earning my own living, and I possess an abundance of vitality and energy wherewith to accomplish it. There is a something inside me telling me it is for my good to be doing something that will provide both income and independence to enable me to enjoy city life."

"That sounds most admirable, Clara. Do you have a profession in mind?"

"Therein lies the quandary I find myself. There must be some kind of business that a woman can undertake, but there exists a masculine monopoly on such opportunities, rendering it difficult for a woman to establish herself. Annoyingly, this is due to the social atmosphere which surrounds us, rather than that woman's capacity."

"I cannot agree more with you, Clara. So recognizing the inability to change the social condition of women, my wisdom has been to make the best of it."

"What do you mean?" Clara was intrigued.

"To be sure, woman in her present status is not fitted to undertake many kinds of business. Her manner of dress, and other habits, would make them rather inconvenient for her. However, her graceful appearance in the eyes of the other sex does provide her with unique opportunities." She slid a calling card across the table. The imprinted name was Madame Q. "This is my business."

Clara tried hard to prevent her mouth from smiling as she took the card, recalling a book she had read in Herbert Chester's library. She looked up. "You are a lady of pleasure?"

"Oh, more than that."

Clara turned the card over and read the business name, The Nunnery, under which was listed an address. "Do you mean to tell me that you keep a house of that kind?"

"I do indeed, but it is a most exclusive establishment catering only to the top echelon of London society. My ladies and I have a delightful time of it. We are well compensated, and our time is our own."

"Oh, how I should love to know the mysteries of such an establishment."

"That you can easily do. Come and spend tonight with us. You shall see everything without being seen yourself. I have a number of beautiful ladies living with me, and every one of them will be gloriously embraced tonight. The rooms are so arranged that we can see everything that transpires in them. Do say that you will come."

"I will be there," Clara responded, unable to conceal her anticipation. "You may depend on it."

AT THE APPOINTED HOUR Clara knocked at the front door of The Nunnery, where Anna met her and bade her inside. "You have just come in time," she said. "For Maria has just taken Albert Hardwood to her room. She is one of the most lascivious girls I have ever known, so I have no doubt we shall bear witness to great fun."

Anna led Clara upstairs and ushered her into a closet which communicated with the adjoining room. Maria and her friend were already there.

Clara was struck with the beauty of the couple. The girl had intensely black hair and eyes, which appeared to be lighted up with desire and passion. Her bust, which her low-necked dress allowed to be seen, was truly magnificent. Her companion was a handsome fellow in his thirties.

"Well, darling," said Albert, pressing her voluptuous bosom close to him, "I have come to see you again. The thoughts of once more tasting the delights of your lovely person has kept me in a continued state of excitement all day. My staff is already in a state of the fiercest erection."

"Let me have oracular demonstrations of the fact," said Maria, opening his pantaloons in front. Out jumped his member, stiff and erect as a poker.

"Oh you naughty boy," she continued, taking his member in her hand and rubbing it up and down. How gloriously stiff you are. I must kiss you, you bad child." So saying, she took his member in her mouth and rolled her tongue over it, while at the same time tickling his testicles.

"Great God!" he cried. "This is too much. I shall spend, dear girl, if you do not cease. All my blood is in a flame."

"It is so delicious, I hate to give it up," she responded, giving it a last kiss. "But I am excited as much as yourself. Slip your hand underneath my petticoats and feel how stiff my clitoris is."

Albert lifted up her skirts, took possession of Maria's luscious cunt with his hand, and proceeded to locate the little sentinel as stiff and firm as his own lance. By his motions, it was clear to Clara that he was rubbing it between his fingers.

"Oh, so delightful," said Maria, a shudder running through her frame. "It is too much. Let me open my thighs a little wider. There, that is much better. Now you can handle my slit a great deal easier. Rub my clitoris harder and titillate the interior of my pussy with your other finger."

"Gladly, darling," He replied. "But, your petticoats are in the way. I want to observe my finger entering in and out of your luscious grotto."

"I will soon remedy that," she replied, lifting her petticoats above her navel, thus exposing her magnificent thighs, a portion of her white belly, and above all, her delicious cunt.

"How beautifully you are made, dear Maria," said Albert, devouring with his eyes the luscious sight before him. "What a luscious belly, and then this masterpiece of nature, this splendid bushy mound. What words can I find to express the beauty of this luscious little quim. How deliciously the lips pout, so inviting to a visitor." Albert seated himself on the ground between Maria's thighs. "Let me examine the interior of this abode of happiness."

With the fingers of one hand Albert opened the lips of Maria's slit and peered curiously into the ruby cavity. He passed the other hand behind her, molding and pressing her buttocks, even advancing one finger into the narrow passage adjacent to the haven of love. He then inserted his tongue between her labia lips, titillated the interior of her grotto, and sucked her clitoris.

Maria was almost mad with pleasure, and showed it by opening her thighs to the widest extent. "Stop, dear Albert," she panted, throwing her arms around his neck when she felt his tongue come in contact with her clitoris. "Or I shall indeed spend. Oh darling, darling. For heaven's sake, stop."

"It is a hard matter to leave the interior of your luscious grotto," Albert told her he withdrew his tongue from her slit and looked into her face. "The sensitive folds of your vagina embraced my tongue so deliciously, and your clitoris is so beautiful, that I hate to give it up. But, darling, let me now see your beautiful breasts."

"How fond you are of molding and pressing a woman's breasts," responded Maria, unhooking her dress and shaking it off her shoulders, thus exposing her magnificently developed globes. "Then here they are. Do what you like with them. See how stiff and firm the nipples stand out."

Albert then began to toy with her breasts, caressing and pressing them, and then sucking their rosy nipples.

While he was thus engaged, Maria once again took possession of his staff of love, capping and uncapping its large ruby head.

"This is too beautiful," said Albert, burying his head between her breasts. "I can contain myself no longer. Come dearest, I must embrace you now. You see how eager my member is to enter your delicious cunt."

"I assure you my slit is not less eager to receive it. Dear Albert, I burn for you. Come, my dear angel. Come. Embrace me. Bury this delicious instrument into the deepest recesses of my vagina." Maria half reclined herself on the sofa and opened her thighs to the widest extent. "Do not spare me. Push it in to the very hilt, make your testicles knock against my bottom. Come, darling, into me quick." She then divided the lips of her pussy with a finger of each hand and revealed the interior of her ruby grotto. "See, I hold open the portals for you. Now you have a fair mark. Come darling, come."

Albert rushed between her thighs, and passing one arm around her neck, brought his instrument to the entrance of her slit. Maria placed one of her feet on the table standing close by the sofa, thus stretching her thighs as widely apart as possible. In another moment he was plunged to the very hilt in her body.

"There, dear girl, you have it now," Albert announced when his instrument was clasped by the lips of her coral sheath. "Oh, how deliciously hot your vagina is! Oh, how tightly your lovely cunt clasps my penis. Your charming breasts, how delightfully they beat against my chest. Stay, I must suck those rosy peaks once more." He continued, bending forward and took one of the strawberry nipples in his mouth, while at the same time continuing his energetic thrusts. "There, how heavenly. How delicious. How exquisite."

"It is too much, darling," Maria almost screamed out, throwing her legs around his loins. "Closer, closer still. Look in the mirror and see how deliciously your penis fills my vagina. I will raise my thighs a little and you will see it better then. There, now you see it. How lusciously it enters in and out of my cavity. I can see it now, but then it is lost in the hair covering my mound."

Their motions increased rapidly, Albert giving violent thrusts and Maria meeting him with corresponding motions of her buttocks.

Oh! Oh! I can stand no more," she continued, wiggling her buttocks. "Dear love, I spend, I come. Oh! Oh—."

"I too am coming, dear Maria."

As the climax approached they seemed crazed with excitement, and at the moment of emission their legs and thighs mingled together in confusion.

Clara and Anna had been more than passive inspectors of this scene. During its continuance, Anna had slid her hand beneath Clara's skirt and, having received no objection, with her finger sought to provide relief to Clara's excited feelings. At the moment of their discharge, she too succumbed, being so much overcome that she was compelled to sit down to catch her breath for a few minutes. She looked up at the smiling Anna, who helped ease her to her feet and kissed her affectionately. "Are you enjoying you visit, Clara?" She asked as she backed away.

Clara's quivering mouth was sufficient to provide an affirmative response, and they again took their stations to continue their viewing of the chamber.

Albert was now stretched lengthwise on the sofa. He was perfectly naked and Maria was lying on the top of him, also stark naked. His arm was passed around her loins and he pressed her tightly against his belly. His left hand rested on her shoulder. Her mouth was fixed to his, and her breasts rested on his chest. Her thighs were stretched widely apart and Albert's staff was embedded in Maria's slit.

Her buttocks were elevated high in the air and she moved them energetically. She then gave three convulsive struggles and ended by falling without motion on Albert's belly. At that moment, Clara saw semen trickle down her thighs.

"They have done for the night," Anna whispered. "Come with me and I will show you something else. For I will be very much mistaken if Rose has not a visitor by this time."

Anna led Clara from their place of concealment and entered a similar apartment at the other end of the corridor. They entered a closet in this room and peered through some cracks in the boarding into the next apartment.

Clara saw a very pretty little plump girl entirely naked on her hands and knees on the bed, presenting her delicious white buttocks with her lovely slit, shaded with brown hair between them. Behind her was a tall, fine looking man, about forty years of age, also naked. In his hand was a birch with which he was gently tickling the lovely girl's bottom.

"What does this mean?" Clara asked.

"That girl you see there is Rose," Anna replied. "Nothing gives her so much pleasure as to be soundly whipped on the bottom by her lover. They always begin in this way. Her companion is Sir George Carlston, a very rich gentlemen. But watch them and you will see something amusing."

Looking again, Clara saw that George was now using the rod a little more freely than when she had first looked. Already the cheeks of Rose's buttocks were turned to a glowing hue, and his instrument was so stiff that it stood boldly up against his belly.

"Harder, George," murmured Rose, her face buried in the pillow. "I scarcely feel it, harder my dear boy, flog me harder."

George obeyed her wishes and let fall a shower of cuts on her plump backside. He continued this for a minute or two, when he suddenly threw down the rod and rushed to her. Instead of entering her by the legitimate road, however, he entered her anally, and passing his hand in front of her, buried two of his fingers in her hairy mound. Every thrust of his buttocks sent his fingers deeper into her vagina, obviously giving her intense delight. Clara then saw her put her hand between her own lily-white thighs and tickle his testicles. It immediately brought on an emission from both of them, and they sank exhausted on the bed.

In the next chamber Clara was shown a somewhat different scene. A beautiful girl, entirely naked, was seated on a low ottoman with her lovely thighs stretched widely apart. Her lover was kneeling on the floor before her and was caressing her lovely cunt with his tongue. It entered in and out her ruby sheath, the lips of which appeared to caress it lovingly. This act alone was sufficient to make him discharge copiously at the same moment that his tongue made her dissolve in bliss.

In another chamber a couple appeared to relish giving themselves manual pleasure instead of the act itself. A lovely girl reclined on the bed with nothing but her chemise on, but still having her breasts and the lower portion of her body bare. Her companion lay by her side with his fingers embedded in her slit, while she had hold of his instrument. They moved their hands together while he tickled her bottom with his other hand. A few rapid motions caused ejaculate to fly from his staff, and he drew his finger dripping from her vagina at the same moment.

It was now growing late and the house was about to close for the night. "Well, Clara. What do you think of The Nunnery?" Anna asked. "The ladies who reside here do so because it suits their pleasure to do so, and their days are their own to do with as they wish. I provide them with room and board and an annual salary of a hundred pounds per year."

"A hundred pounds?" Clara gasped.

"Three or four times the wages of a governess, eh?" Anna grinned. "Yes Clara. As Madame Q, I am offering you a position here. You are a very pretty girl, well-bred and educated, and so are precisely what the gentlemen who come here are seeking."

"I, I don't know what to say." Clara was clearly overwhelmed.

"Say nothing for now." Madame Q placed her right index finger across Clara's lips. "Sleep on it."

Chapter Five: A Lady of Pleasure

Clara's acceptance of Madame Q's offer was almost a given, but she did have questions before she formally accepted it. Role play was going to be new to her, but Madame Q explained that she would be able to define which roles she wished to participate in. She would have no problem with performing with other ladies, an activity frequently requested by clients. In fact, she rather relished that aspect. Gentlemen would have previously defined activities prior to coming to her room so she would always know what she was to do, but Madame Q explained that Clara was free to negotiate further activities directly with a client. And any 'gifts' he bestowed upon her in return were hers to keep. It seemed that such gifts more than doubled the annual salaries for most of the ladies.

The Nunnery was a huge house in a fashionable part of London, and it took Clara most of her first day to learn the layout.

The rear entrance was for servants and tradesmen. Also in the back of the house was a stairway leading to the attic and all floors, which was how the servants moved around unseen. This was called the servant stairway.

Downstairs were the kitchen, scullery, pantry and both the housekeeper and cook had their rooms there. The remainder of the staff's had garret rooms in the attic.

The main foyer of the house featured the grand staircase, to the right of which was the dining room where Madame Q, her ladies, and sometimes guests, dined. To the left was a large lounge where ladies and clients mingled, and drinks were served here. The staircase itself led to the second floor where the ladies rooms were, and ladies would take clients upstairs to their room using the grand staircase. There were a total of twelve well-furnished apartments. Clara occupied number ten. On the second floor and above were staircases on either side of the house leading to the upper floors.

On the third floor was Madame Q's bedroom, 5 rooms which could be used as guest rooms, where a gentleman may also keep a mistress who would be treated as a guest, or for temporary use as dolly mop or virgin rooms; these were girls who did not permanently reside in the house. Also on this floor was the library.

The fourth floor had been converted to four specialty rooms. One was a well-appointed 'dungeon' with shackles on the wall and hooks on the ceiling. Another was a comfortable room with a spanking horse, which was Madame Q's room for her birching club. The other two rooms were available for private parties and were appointed accordingly.

Over the next week, Clara spent time getting to know the other ladies, who not only welcomed her and made her feel comfortable, but also gave her ideas for possible role plays and activities which may boost her purse. Madame Q then began to introduce her to The Nunnery's clientele, and the next day Clara was initiated into becoming a lady of pleasure with her first role play scene. She was to play an 'innocent' girl who meets a man in the library.

Clara entered the library rather suddenly and found Roger Percival deeply engaged in a book. When he saw her, he hastily endeavored to conceal the volume.

"What are you reading, Mr. Percival?" Clara asked sweetly.

"Something that I cannot show you, Miss Clara," he replied.

"Nonsense," Clara giggled. "You need not be afraid, for I believe I can look at anything."

"You will not be angry or offended if I show you this book?" he exclaimed.

"Certainly not, for I do wish to see it. And rest assured that whatever it may contain will neither offend me nor shock me."

"Then take it and judge for yourself," he answered, then after a moment's pause he added, "What say you?"

"Oh, sir. I relish being initiated in the mysteries contained within this book."

"Ah, Clara," said Roger, kissing her and forcing his tongue into her mouth. "I perceive you may soon be as fond of amorous sports as I am. I foresee some delicious pleasures together." He pressed Clara's palpitating bosom to his, kissing her in the same manner as before.

"Dear Roger," she replied, returning his caresses by imitating his actions, and advancing her tongue to meet his. "I am yours to teach."

"Bravely spoken, Clara," returned Roger. "But come, darling, take me into your bed chamber where we might proceed in comfort."

Clara led the way to her private room. It was neatly furnished, and was replete with every luxury. A carpet soft as velvet was spread on the floor and capacious sofas, soft and springy, just fitted for the performance of the conjugal act, were placed around the apartment. An immense mirror adorned one of the walls. No light of day was permitted to enter this nest, but it was illuminated by means of brilliant gas burners, and a perfume of the most intoxicating description was distilled through the atmosphere.

Once they entered her apartment a delicious languor stole over Clara. She threw herself into Roger's arms, squeezing, kissing, and even biting him. He returned her embraces with as much ardor as her own. She then placed her hand outside his trousers and felt his stiff instrument.

"Stop, darling," he told her. "These clothes are in the way, and I should love to feel your hand on my naked staff." He began to undress, and in a few moments he was entirely in a state of nature. Clara rushed to him and kissed his naked body all over. He shivered in her arms, and would have discharged right then had he not torn himself from her embrace. "Now, Clara," he said, wagging his index finger at her. "It is nothing but fair that you should let me see you also naked."

"Dearest Roger, do with me as you will. My whole body is yours."

"Bless you, darling, I only hope I may be able to satisfy you to your heart's content," he said as he tore off her clothes, reducing her to a perfect state of nudity. He then led her to a sofa and reclined her onto it, then stood a few feet off that he might better observe her naked beauties. "What glorious beauty," he exclaimed delightedly. "How magnificently formed your body is, dear Clara. What well developed thighs and perfect straight legs you have. And, oh, your delicious cunt. Open your thighs a little, dear Clara, that I may enjoy a better view of it."

"Like this?" Clara complied obediently.

"Yes, that's it. Now I can see it perfectly. How inviting the lips look amidst your downy hair. How closely they fold together showing a line of coral between them! Oh, how I long to taste the sweets of that delicious grotto." He rubbed his hands together. "Now, dear Clara, turn on your belly, and elevate your buttocks a little. There, that's it exactly. Great heavens, the back of the picture is even more glorious than the front. What a delicious bottom. How closely the cheeks come together."

Clara could stand no more, and jumping up from the sofa she rushed into his arms. "Dearest Roger, give me relief or I shall die."

Roger then began to kiss what he had admired. He pressed Clara to himself and embraced her breasts, her belly, her bottom and then her mound of Venus. The contact of the warm flesh inflamed their passions. They squirmed and wiggled in each other's arms, hugging and kissing, until they rolled on the floor. Then, interlacing their thighs, Roger's staff touched Clara's cunt. She rolled herself on the top of him, forcing him inside her, and moved backwards and forwards as he placed a hand on each cheek of her bottom and pressed her slit down to his testicles. A convulsive shudder ran through both their frames and they closed their eyes in the ecstasy of sensations, and they both discharged profusely.

When they had rested some little time, Clara went to a recess and took from it a delicious cordial. They both partook freely, and it had the effect of completely restoring their energies. They commenced touching and titillations, and were soon in a glorious state of desire again.

"Clara, my darling," Roger commenced. "Lie down on the sofa again, I want to manipulate your charms a little more at my ease. We were so carried away by our feelings that we discharged before we had sufficiently prolonged our pleasures. Let us be more prudent this time."

Acting upon his instruction, Clara laid down on the sofa. Roger seated himself on an ottoman by her side and commenced to excite her with his caresses. Fastening himself on the first instance on her breasts, he sucked her nipples, and tickled her under her arms. Then, following this tribute of admiration to her bust, he straddled her chest and brought his instrument and testicles directly over her two ivory globes. He then rubbed his staff and pendants against her breasts. Then pressed them closely together with his engine nestled between them. His buttocks quivered with delight. "Oh, Clara," he told her. "How delicious your breasts feel to me. I could almost fancy it was its own proper nest," he added while continuing to move his buttocks backwards and forwards. He seemed about to spend, but dismounted in order to prevent that occurrence and took a seat by Clara's side on the sofa.

His hand then descended to Clara's slit where he made a full stop. A convulsive thrill ran through his body when his hand came in contact with the hair adorning her mound and he entwined it in his fingers, gently pulling it, just enough to provide Clara with the most pleasing titillation without giving her the slightest pain. He then invaded the sanctuary of love itself, gently dividing the lips and advancing two fingers into her vagina. After allowing them to rest there a few moments, he pushed further in until they were wholly engulfed in her hot, wet passage. "Oh, Clara," he exclaimed, moving his fingers in and out of her slit. I will soon be ready bury my staff into this lovely cavity."

"Darling," Clara replied. "Your touches almost take away my senses. For heaven's sake stop, or I shall spend. I shall indeed."

"I understand, my darling, but it must not be yet." Roger withdrew his fingers from her vagina and carried it to the top of her slit and tickled her clitoris. "There now," he said. "I have the little sentinel between my fingers. How soft it is," he said, rubbing it gently.

During these manipulations on his part, Clara proceeded to pay him back in his own coin. Rubbing his staff in her hand, she caused him to him squirm and wriggle again.

"Clara, I am going to give you a glorious embracing, and if I don't make you spend as you have never spent before, I shall be very much deceived. I intend to treat your delicious little cunt to the most vigorous of fucking. Now, Clara, on your back. Open your thighs, and let me engulf my staff in your salacious slit."

Clara excitedly threw herself onto her back and Roger was on the top of her in a moment. A mere second later his prick was soundly embedded into her wanting cunt.

Clara moaned with delight, experiencing intense pleasure, while Roger pounded his instrument in and out of her, sucking her breasts and holding her hands in his above her head. He finally froze and she felt his pulsing member discharge inside her, thus finishing the business. With a cry of joy, Clara once again entered into the throes of delicious orgasm.

THERE WAS A KNOCK AT Clara's door half an hour after Roger had left. It was Madame Q. "Roger Percival told me you are the most delightful girl he has ever had pleasure with," she told Clara. "And he will henceforth become a frequent visitor of yours. Congratulations. You have your first admirer. You are going to do very well here."

"Were you in the next door closet?" Clara asked, suddenly realized for the first time that her employer had more than likely been watching the proceedings.

"But of course." Madame Q gave Clara a reassuring smile. "And a most splendid performance it was, too."

THE END

About the Author

With keen interest in nineteenth and early twentieth century history, Dorian Shellan writes a variety of stories with Victorian settings.

The Victorian era was one of great innovations, industrial, medical, and social. Dorian's stories incorporate many of these changes and the impact it had on the population of that time.

Dorian's genres range from novels, including adventure and romance, to short stories, to Victorian erotica.

Read more at https://victorianstories.com.

www.ingramcontent.com/pod-product-compliance
Lightning Source LLC
LaVergne TN
LVHW050610100826
845148LV00015B/3213

* 9 7 8 1 6 3 7 8 6 0 3 2 8 *